To Ariana and Alexander

Color-Aid and Strathmore watercolor papers were used for the full-color illustrations. Photography of cut-paper illustrations by Studio One.
The text type is 17-point Symbol ITC Medium.

Copyright © 1998 by David Wisniewski

Published by Lothrop, Lee & Shepard Books
an imprint of Morrow Junior Books
a division of William Morrow and Company, Inc.
1350 Avenue of the Americas, New York, NY 10019
http://www.williammorrow.com

Printed in Singapore at Tien Wah Press.

2 3 4 5 6 7 8 9 10

Library of Congress Cataloging-in-Publication Data
Wisniewski, David.
The secret knowledge of grown-ups/revealed and illustrated by David Wisniewski.
p. cm.
Summary: A humorous revelation of the real reasons why adults tell children to do things, such as "Eat your vegetables," "Comb your hair," and "Don't blow bubbles in your milk."
ISBN 0-688-15339-9 (trade)—ISBN 0-688-15340-2 (library)
1. Children—Humor. 2. Adulthood—Humor. [1. Behavior—Wit and humor.] I. Title. PN6231.C32W57 1998 818'.5402—dc21
97-6469 CIP AC

THE SECRET KNOWLEDGE OF GROWN-UPS

Revealed and illustrated by

David Wisniewski

LOTHROP, LEE & SHEPARD BOOKS • MORROW

NEW YORK

The truth must be told to kids!

For too long, for centuries in fact, it's been covered over, hidden, impossible to find. A conspiracy, an organized silence by generations of grown-ups, has kept the truth from millions of children throughout history.

"And what is this truth?" you ask.

Simply this: The reasons grown-ups tell you to do things are not true!

"Eat your vegetables," they say.

"Why?" you ask.

"They're good for you," they reply.

NONSENSE!

"Comb your hair," they say.

"Why?" you ask.

"It keeps it neat," they reply.

POPPYCOCK!

There are far more sinister, truly macabre reasons for these seemingly innocent requests. As a parent, I went along with it all at first: going to secret meetings, memorizing huge volumes of lies and falsehoods, preparing for the day when my kids would want to know why this and why that.

But not anymore!

Over the last three years, I've gathered as much information as I could: crisscrossing the country in clever, impenetrable disguises, breaking into the secret files kept by hundreds of grown-ups, assembling the evidence. And now it's here, in your hands.

It's the truth. It's real. It's...

I must go. They're coming. I can hear them. Quickly! Take this book! Read it! LEARN THE TRUTH!!!

LOCATION:
American Produce Council
Aurora, Illinois

DATE & TIME: July 22, 1997
1:30 P.M.

LOG: Enter A.P.C. compound
in vegetable truck, posing as
large eggplant. Break into file
room during lunch. Discover
GROWN-UP RULE #31! Escape
through crowded cafeteria,
claiming to be leftover
moussaka.

TOP SECRET

CLASSIFIED
SECURITY
CLEARANCE A

GROWN-UP RULE #31:

Eat your vegetables.

OFFICIAL REASON:

They're good for you.

THE TRUTH:

You don't eat vegetables because they're good for you. You eat vegetables to k...

to keep them under control!

Millions of years ago, vegetables ruled the earth. Big bunches of broccoli stomped through the jungles, followed by ferocious carrots and savage packs of peas. Huge heads of lettuce roamed the grasslands and giant celery stalked the plains.

And what were these terrible vegetables looking for?

You guessed it.... People! Yes, these were meat-eating vegetables.

They terrorized the early humans, attacking without warning. Our ancestors put up with this for centuries, living in drafty caves and getting nasty head colds. But then they discovered sticks and stones.

With these new weapons, humans began to defend themselves. At first, lone hunters would take on a single radish or green bean. Eventually, groups of hunters tackled bigger game, like the saber-toothed asparagus and woolly cucumber. By mixing these vanquished vegetables, primitive chefs invented salad.

The real turning point, however, was the discovery of fire. With it, hunters could frighten the less intelligent vegetables into ambushes and traps.

Thousands of butternut squash, frightened by hunters' fiery torches, plunge over a cliff in what is now France. Scientists believe this incident gave squash its name.

Courageous humans confront a fully grown cornasaur, using their torches to fatally overheat the beast's vital kernels.

More important, fire allowed humans to cook their leafy foes. As this fossil from Montana shows, predatory potatoes and man-eating mushrooms were turned into Stone Age casseroles.

This brought the Age of Vegetables to a close. As the human race grew in size and intelligence, vegetables became smaller and dumber, devolving into the pathetic produce of gardens and grocery stores.

| 1,000,000 B.C. | 100,000 B.C. | 8,000 B.C. | 3,000 B.C. | TODAY |

To prevent vegetables from ever regaining power, grown-ups eat them. They don't like the flavor any more than you do, but it keeps the little horrors fearful and demoralized. It's a simple way to protect modern civilization.

Besides, which would you rather do: eat vegetables or be eaten by vegetables?

LOCATION: United Dairies Corporation
Des Moines, Iowa

DATE & TIME: July 31, 1997, 11:30 P.M.

LOG: Disguised as Polled Guernsey, lead herd of cows into high-security area. During melee, locate *GROWN-UP RULE #37!* Abandon disguise, disappointing bull. Close call.

TOP SECRET

CLASSIFIED

SECURITY CLEARANCE A

GROWN-UP RULE #37:

Drink plenty of milk.

OFFICIAL REASON:

It's good for you.

THE TRUTH:

Yes, milk is packed with vitamins and protein, but that's not why parents want you to drink it. The real reason is

...to stop our atomic cows from exploding!

Kids have been told that millions of cows produce our country's milk. That's not true. At this moment, only five giant cows do all the work. The others are decoys made of plywood and old box springs.

One of these colossal cows is Flossie. Eighty feet tall, she provides the daily milk supply for Utah, Nevada, Wyoming, and Colorado. Flossie is kept under tight security at a secret air-force base, right next to the hangar where they stack all the banged-up flying saucers.

Flossie's size is no accident. In the 1950s, our government was afraid that the Russians would develop the first atomic cow and flood the market with Communist milk. To prevent this, American scientists fed Flossie and her friends radioactive hay.

ATOMIC COW REGIONAL SITES

Flossie
(Wyoming)

Pittypat
(New York)

Bluebell
(California)

Bonnie
(Wisconsin)

Doris
(Arizona)

Enid
(Tennessee)

The experiment worked great, and government officials are very happy that all this milk is available. But they worry about one thing: Flossie can't be turned off. The milk just keeps coming.

For this reason, all atomic cow sites are equipped with extra milking machines. For backup, glass cases on the wall contain emergency farmers with really big hands.

However, there is one crisis the government can't prepare for: kids *not* drinking milk. If that happened, Flossie would have to hold it,

Oscar Larsen served as an emergency milker for the Wisconsin Atomic Cow Project, spending eighteen years in a glass case. "You learn a lot in a place like that," said Larsen. "I just can't remember what it was."

getting bigger and bigger until—*nuclear milkdown*!

Such a catastrophe forever scars the landscape between the Arizona towns of Flagstaff and Winslow. A huge crater is all that remains of Doris, the only atomic cow that ever exploded.

When kids felt the ground shake and saw the curdled cloud of dairy products form over the desert back in 1962, they were told that a meteor had hit the local Tastee Freeze.

Now you know better. So drink your milk.

LOCATION:
Jenkins Barber College
Baltimore, Maryland

DATE & TIME: October 12, 1997
8:30 A.M.

LOG: Penetrate facility
concealed under toupee of
unsuspecting dean. Find
GROWN-UP RULE #42 in coat
pocket! Slip off dean's head,
disguised as dandruff.

TOP SECRET

CLASSIFIED
SECURITY CLEARANCE A

GROWN-UP RULE #42:

Comb your hair.

OFFICIAL REASON:

It keeps it neat.

THE TRUTH:

You don't comb your hair to keep it neat. You comb your hair

to stop it from going back into those little holes in your head!

Yes, that's right! Hair doesn't grow out. Hair grows *in*! Why else would you pull it around with a comb? After all, you only pull things when they want to go the other way.

Within the scalp, thousands of powerful sumo cells drag individual hairs into the head. The hair passes through the skull (which protects the brain from shock) after traveling through a layer of fat (which protects the brain from thinking).

Skull

Brain

The proof of Reverse Hair Growth (RHG) can be found in the following time-lapse photography of a newborn baby. Notice that the infant arrives with an abundance of hair. This is *entirely normal*. Then the sumo cells begin their lifelong work.

11:27:04 11:27:11 11:27:18

Within moments, a short-haired baby is presented to gullible brothers and sisters, who stroke the baby's head, thereby preventing complete baldness.

Because most girls brush and comb their hair a lot, they don't have to worry much about Reverse Hair Growth. Boys do, not only because they don't comb much, but also because many get very short haircuts. RHG happens so fast, a flattop or crew cut can grow back into a guy's head in one night!

Luckily, there are two ways to avoid this danger:

1. *Blow on your thumb.* This raises your body's air pressure and creates internal wind gusts of seventy-five MPH, forcing sumo cells to release the hair shafts.

Do not be alarmed if you hear a slight whistling noise when you do this; it is only extra air coming out your ears.

2. *Chew gum.* Microscopic gum molecules find their way to the inside of your head, where they stick to the sumo cells for at least forty-eight hours. Chewing more gum will extend this time.

But what if you get really careless and don't comb your hair and it all grows back inside your head? Two things will happen:

1. *You will be bald.*

2. *Your head will be stuffed with ingrown hair.*

This doesn't leave much room for brains. Then you will be bald and kind of stupid.

However, all is not lost. Nature is wonderful and takes care of Cranial Hair Overload (CHO) in a couple of great ways:

1. *It directs the hair to grow someplace else.*

This is why so many bald guys have beards and mustaches. It is a known fact that William Shakespeare sprouted a mustache and goatee to alleviate the brain crowding caused by CHO.

2. *It relocates the brain to a place that has more room, like a briefcase or a hat.*

For instance, British leader Winston Churchill kept his brain in a bowler hat for many years, then switched it to a bomb-proof briefcase when World War II began.

The next time you spot a bald guy, see if he wears a beard, a mustache, or a hat, or if he carries a briefcase. If he does, chances are he's pretty smart. If not, talk slowly and don't use any big words, because he's probably a dope.

LOCATION: Niftee Straw Factory
Cranston, Missouri

DATE & TIME: November 8, 1997, 6:15 P.M.

LOG: Enter premises within chocolate milk shake. Find *GROWN-UP RULE #56* in storeroom! Flippers stick to floor; must leave behind. Security arrives. I roll on carpet, picking up lint. Make getaway as giant fuzz ball.

TOP SECRET

CLASSIFIED

SECURITY CLEARANCE A

GROWN-UP RULE #56:

Don't blow bubbles in your milk.

OFFICIAL REASON:

It's noisy, sloppy, and rude.

THE TRUTH:

Those aren't the real reasons. The truth is that blowing the wrong way down a straw reverses the molecular action, creating a powerful vacuum

th t sucks your f c right into the glass!

Kids don't know it, but thousands of these incidents happen every year. That's why all grown-ups keep an Emergency Suckface Kit with a hammer and crowbar within easy reach of the dinner table, where most milk-related accidents occur. Unfortunately, a quick rescue seldom prevents the hideous result of having your face sucked into a glass.

Because of their unusual features, suckfaced survivors once faced cruel taunts and demeaning careers of licking stamps and blowing up balloons. However, recent advances in face masks have allowed many of the afflicted to reenter society. As these dramatic before and after photographs show, many talented, prominent citizens have returned to lead fulfilling and productive lives.

| Albert Einstein | Elvis Presley | Pablo Picasso | Groucho Marx | Richard Nixon |

But why give yourself problems? Don't blow bubbles in milk with a straw. And never, *never* blow bubbles into a soda bottle.

LOCATION: Burgess Cafeteria Supply
Avery, West Virginia

DATE & TIME: December 12, 1997, 2:30 P.M.

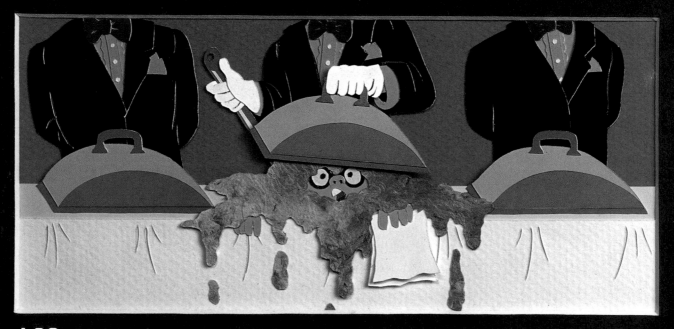

LOG: Camouflaged with bread pudding, enter showroom in steam table. Grab *GROWN-UP RULE #61* when rolling past main office! Injured by slotted spoon. Escape noticeable. Must be more careful.

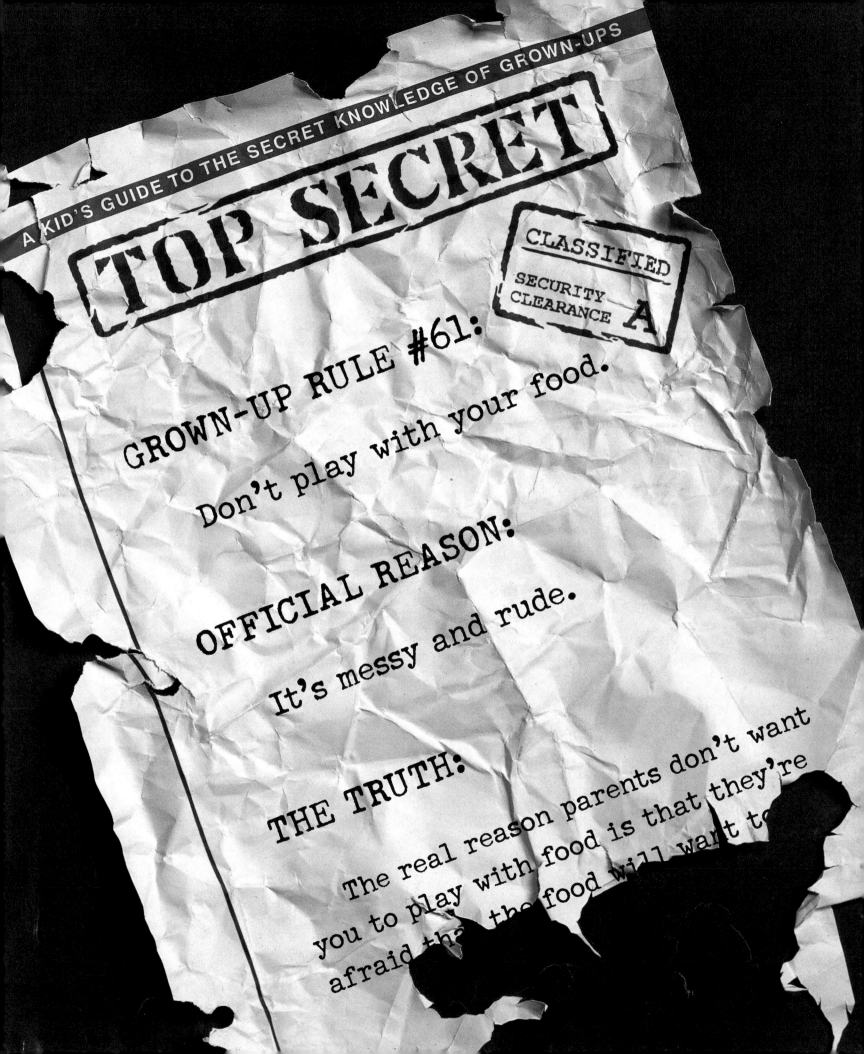

TOP SECRET

CLASSIFIED
SECURITY CLEARANCE A

GROWN-UP RULE #61:

Don't play with your food.

OFFICIAL REASON:

It's messy and rude.

THE TRUTH:

The real reason parents don't want you to play with food is that they're afraid that the food will want to

that the food will want to play with you!

Honestly, it doesn't take much to get food to play. And once it starts, it's almost impossible to stop. That's when things get messy. (The only exception is food from the school cafeteria, which is so depressed about its career that it won't react to anything.)

Even bland foods can be a challenge. Oatmeal keeps playing gin rummy even after the cards stick together. Poached eggs spend so much time on crossword puzzles that the paper falls apart. And applesauce plays checkers long after you can't see the board anymore.

This stubborn playfulness increases with spicy foods. Tacos insist on tag, then get salsa all over the couch. Swedish meatballs beg to play soccer, but always leave gravy on the rug.

Some foods are simply too rough to play with. Fried chicken loves to play chicken. As illustrated above, children and chicken parts rush at each other at high speed until one side moves out of the way. Pork can also be dangerous. Unless thoroughly cooked, it plays this little kiddie went to market, which often ends with sprained toes.

Knowing all this usually stops kids from playing with their food. If not, make sure you wear a helmet and knee pads to dinner. That steak could be tougher than it looks.

LOCATION:
Cozy Comfort Mattress Company
Lorgnette, Oregon

DATE & TIME: January 17, 1998
4:30 A.M.

LOG: Disguised as bedbug, enter loading dock. Find *GROWN-UP RULE #62* in stuffing bin. Get sprayed by janitor. Play dead. Swept up in dustpan. Exit in garbage.

TOP SECRET

CLASSIFIED
SECURITY CLEARANCE **A**

GROWN-UP RULE #62:

Don't jump on your bed.

OFFICIAL REASONS:

You'll break it.
You might get hurt.

THE TRUTH:

Yes, it's possible to break your bed if you jump on it. And it's possible you might get hurt if you fall off. But you'll definitely get hurt

if you wake up the mattress!

You see, mattresses aren't just big lifeless rectangles crammed with stuffing. They are active woolly creatures raised on farms in Scotland.

There, the mattress herders (or mattherds) sing a lovely ballad as their frisky mattdogs guide the beasts to pasture:

Mattresses are bonny things,
  Born of stuffing, cloth, and springs.
Gaily now they graze the meadow,
  Growing soon to be my bed. Oh!
Single, double, queen, and king,
  A flock like this doth make me sing!
Methinks my joy shall never wilt!
  By gar! The beasties just ate my kilt!

After growing to adulthood, the mattresses start a long period of hibernation. Undisturbed by noise and handling, they are rounded up, sorted by size, and sold to stores. Then they end up in your bedroom, where they snooze peacefully year after year. Unless you jump on them. Fortunately, today's mattresses are very difficult to wake up. That wasn't the case with their hardy ancestors.

When the first Scots arrived in Scotland by parcel post more than six thousand years ago, they saw wild mountain mattresses jumping from peak to peak. By imitating the creature's mating call with bagpipes, the Scots tried to capture one. But none succeeded.

Then one night, about A.D. 1040, the Scottish king Malcolm the Upset wandered the moors, trying to get over eating haggis*, a real humdinger of a national dish. He stumbled upon a hibernating mattress, upon which he slept soundly for the first time in many years. When he woke, Malcolm realized that the wild mattress was more comfortable than the boulder he usually slept on.

*haggis: a pudding eaten in Scotland made from the heart, lungs, and liver of a sheep, chopped up and mixed with suet, oatmeal, onions, and spices, and boiled in the stomach of the animal. No, I am *not* making this up!

NOMOR FORME THANX

MALCOLM THE UPSET

King Malcolm brought the mattress home and began breeding it. Soon he was giving mattresses as gifts to other kings and queens. Unfortunately, these feral mattresses woke up and started slinging royalty around, an event immortalized on canvas by court artist Red Harry McLegs, who was five years old at the time.

This was very bad for King Malcolm, who spent the rest of his life in prison, eating haggis. But it was very good for us—we now have the modern domestic mattress with its mild disposition and long hibernation period.

Still, it's not a good idea to jump on your bed. That mattress might be hard to wake up, but it's not impossible.

And, for goodness' sake, don't play the bagpipes near it!

LOCATION:
Dixie's Nail Emporium
Bald Knob, South Dakota

DATE & TIME: February 4, 1998
3:15 P.M.

LOG: Almost complete disaster!
Nail disguise detected
immediately by incredibly
observant staff. Snatch *GROWN-UP
RULE #73* from desk! Pounded into
floor by large woman with big
hammer. Escape through knothole.

TOP SECRET

GROWN-UP RULE #73:

Don't bite your fingernails.

OFFICIAL REASON:

It makes your fingernails look terrible.

THE TRUTH:

Although bitten fingernails really do look pretty terrible, that's not the real reason parents want you to stop. The real reason is the scraps of fingernail you leave behind. Why?

Because

they grow!

Just like carrot seeds become carrots and bean seeds become beans, fingernail scraps become fingers. After growing under your bed or between the sofa pillows for about three months, the new fingers leave their nests and go crawling around the house.

At first, this isn't too much of a problem. With their dimpled knuckles and sunny dispositions, the baby fingers are actually kind of cute. But as they get older, the fingers start behaving badly.

PHONE BILL

$54,000.00

They ring your doorbell and run. They dial long-distance to order anchovy and onion pizza delivered to people you don't know. They swipe the icing off cakes and poke chocolates to find out what the fillings are.

Psychologists think that the fingers act this way because they grow up alone without ever belonging to a hand. Upon adolescence, the fingers form groups to make up for it. And that's the most important reason not to bite your fingernails:

PINKY ♡ POINTY

PIZZA

to stop the spread of teenage finger gangs!

These gangs are based on physical characteristics. They are:

1. *The Stubby Creeps* This band of disturbed thumbs travels by hitchhiking. They get a kick out of making sudden jerky movements and yelling, "Take a hike!" Gang leaders wear black T-shirts with *I'm Opposable!* scrawled on them.

2. *The Pointing Punks* These rebellious forefingers pointlessly scold and accuse people. They are often busted for picking noses that don't belong to them. For laughs, they'll poke you in the eye.

3. *The Dirty Digits*   This bunch of middle fingers just stands around. That's bad enough.

4. *The Ring Leaders*   These boisterous ring fingers spend most of their time showing off flashy jewelry. Unlike members of other gangs, many are engaged or even married.

5. *Hell's Pinkies*   This pathetic group of little fingers tries to imitate the Ring Leaders by wearing jewelry. Psychologists think they do it because they're self-conscious about their height and have rotten jobs cleaning ears.

So do society a favor: Stop biting your fingernails. If you can't break the habit, dispose of the scraps properly by sending them to an accordion factory. They use lone fingers to test accordions because most normal people don't want to listen to them.

LOCATION:
Puffies Tissue Plant
Brookline, Massachusetts

DATE & TIME: March 2, 1998
2:30 P.M.

LOG: Enter plant as tissue
tester. Blow safe. Find
GROWN-UP RULE #82! Quickly
catch cold. Blast to safety
with sneeze.

TOP SECRET

GROWN-UP RULE #82:

Don't pick your nose.

OFFICIAL REASON:

It's gross and disgusting.

THE TRUTH:

Actually, picking your nose is gross and disgusting. However, that's not the real reason, which is

to stop your brain from deflating!

The air pipeline that keeps your brain inflated runs past the nostrils to a vast pumping station inside your head. There, floating majestically from its moorings, linked to thousands of ingrown hairs, is the magnificent human brain, swaying gently in the breeze. Until you stick a finger up your nose.

This intruding digit will certainly dent the pipeline. It may even poke a hole in it, causing an outburst of air called, in technical language, a sneeze. This minor damage is quickly patched by alert mending muscles.

Microphotography captures the horror of helpless mending muscles as the brain of inveterate nosepicker Lindsay Hindenburg of Lakehurst, New Jersey, deflates in spectacular fashion.

More aggressive techniques, such as the use of knuckles or toes, result in complete pipeline failure. Should poking of this magnitude continue, the brain becomes unhooked from the pipeline and deflates.

If you can't give up this nasty habit right away, at least be familiar with the five warning signs of brain deflation:

1. *A faint hissing noise.*
2. *A sound like a balloon let loose in a bathtub.*
3. *A rubbery thumping as your brain flies around.*
4. *Silence.*
5. *A floppy rolling noise when you tilt your head.*

Although this baggy brain still works, it won't absorb much new information, so it pays to fix it before the next spelling test. Here's the simple way:

1. *Shine a flashlight up your nose.*
   Just as a plant turns toward the sun, your brain will be attracted to the light shining up your nose and flop over to it. Your brain will then be centered over the pipeline, ready for inflation.

2. *Hold your nose and hum.*
   Finger pressure stabilizes the pipeline. Humming entertains the mending muscles as they drive bulldozers around to fix things up.

There is a more difficult way to reinflate your brain, but it requires four years of college, one pair of pliers, and three feet of lead pipe.

Hundreds of grown-up rules remain. The truth must be told about THEM ALL! But they're on my trail. I hear them coming. And so for now